Heidi's Hounds

Book 1: The Sick Puppy

Carey V. Azzara

Published by Glass Spider Publishing

www.glassspiderpublishing.com

ISBN 9781090341389

Library of Congress Control Number: 2019937779

Cover design by Judith S. Design & Creativity

www.judithsdesign.com

Art/illustrations by Garcia Thompson

Edited by Vince Font

To my darling daughter, who saved Mato's life, giving birth to this story.

Contents

Chapter 1: An Unexpected Change

Heidi skipped home, filled with the anticipation of summer. A sturdy seven-year-old, she loved her home in the town of Cumberland, Maine. Her family's ranch-style house was nestled in a friendly neighborhood a few blocks from Mabel I. Wilson Elementary School. Heidi walked there every day. But soon she'd be home on vacation, which meant playing outside, trips to the beach, and lots of swimming and fishing.

"Hey, Mom, I'm home!" Heidi grabbed an apple, and with a mouthful of fruit, said, "Gonna do my homework now."

"All right dear. I'll call you when dinner is ready."

Faint purple walls, with an eight-inch lobster border of wallpaper that wrapped around the bedroom, reflected Heidi's cheerful nature. Her bed had a white frame, a carved backboard, and high, rounded posts in all four corners. The room was littered with stuffed animals, books, pictures, fishing gear, and clothes. She sat at her desk in the far corner of the room where her dad had built a triangular work space.

Surprised to hear the automatic door opener cranking in the attached garage, Heidi put down her pencil. Why would her dad be home so early? She decided to investigate. She went down the hall and peered into the kitchen.

Her dad burst through the back door. He wore a broad smile on his face but said nothing.

"You're home early," Helen, his wife, said.

Heidi's dad was about to respond but stopped when he noticed Heidi peeking around a corner. "Hey, Heidi-o, how's it goin'?" he said. "Looking forward to summer, I'll bet." He turned toward Helen. "Yeah, I knocked off early. Thought I'd get a jump on the weekend."

He tried to act casual, but his excitement betrayed him; both Heidi and Helen knew something was up. Wisely, Helen went along with his cover story. Heidi gave her dad a hug before heading back to finish her school work. As she left, she watched her dad wrap his arm around her mom and give her a big kiss.

"What's that for?" Helen asked, smiling. Then, glancing down the hall, "Okay, Heidi is gone. Spill the beans."

"You'll never guess what happened today," Greg said, then paused.

"So tell me already."

"I received a call early this afternoon from that company in Virginia. You know, the one I told you about." He stopped and gave her a Cheshire grin.

"C'mon, tell me. What did they say?"

"They wanna hire me. They'll pay all our moving expenses, and . . . get this . . . I'll be making almost *twice* what I make now. Of course, living expenses are higher in Virginia, but it's a great opportunity."

"Oh my gosh!" Helen exclaimed. "Let me sit down."

"Well, what do you think? What should we tell them?"

"It's terrific news, dear. I just don't know what to say. I mean, leaving our friends and uprooting Heidi . . . there's a lot to consider."

"Yes, yes, you're right," Greg said. "We should weigh all the pluses and minuses. Let's not tell Heidi until we decide. No point in getting her upset."

"Yes," Helen said, "we should sleep on it. No need to worry Heidi if we decide not to go."

But it was too late. Heidi had heard every word. Their small house had heating vents that also acted as a means for Heidi to spy on her parents. Long ago, she learned to listen whenever they discussed things she wasn't privy to.

The next day, Heidi was up and ready for school without being asked. Her mother gave her a quizzical glance, but Heidi ignored her. "I want to get to school early," Heidi said.

"All right dear. Perhaps this afternoon we can go shopping for a new bathing suit. I doubt the one we bought last year will fit. You've grown so much."

Heidi knew her parents would be making their decision, and although she wanted to know, she also didn't want to know . . . you know?

Daydreams about moving affected her attention all day, but finally the last bell rang and school was over until Monday. The walk home was short, and Heidi was always happy for it, especially in winter. But today, she wished she lived ten miles away. "I guess stalling won't make it any easier," she said to herself. "Might as well face it."

A slow, deliberate climb up the front steps ended in an abrupt halt when Heidi saw the front door ajar. She poked her head in tentatively.

"Hello?"

"It's okay, sweetie, come in," her mom said. "I left the door open for you. We want to discuss something with you. Please sit down and just listen so we can explain, okay?" Her parents glanced at one another.

But before Helen could speak, Heidi, still standing, exploded, "We're going to live in Virginia!" Her parents' eyes widened with surprise. "Yeah, I know all about it. Dad got a terrific new job," Heidi said in a nasty sing-song manner. "Does anyone ever care about what I want?"

She hadn't planned to make a fuss, but it all came crashing down around her. She raced down the hall to her bedroom and slammed her bedroom door behind her.

"I should go to her," Helen said.

"No, wait," Greg said. "Give her some space. I'll talk with her after dinner."

Chapter 2: New Places and People

School ended for the summer, and the Morgan family made ready for their move south. Heidi's dad had sold the house and found a home in Virginia near a good elementary school. They were going to live on Tancreti Lane in Alexandria, Virginia, in a neighborhood where the homes were mostly townhouses two and three stories high. The house they bought had a beautiful flowering tree in the front yard. It gave Heidi hope.

But everything was different: townhouses rather than standalone homes, lots and lots of people, kids, dogs, plus cars everywhere—and the noise. Heidi wondered how she'd be able to think to do school work with all the noise.

This will take getting used to, she lamented.

Samuel W. Tucker Elementary School was close by, and although it was closed for the summer, Heidi took a walk over to get a feel for the place.

The building seemed pleasant enough, with a friendly white entry and walls of warm red brick.

"It's going to be a lonely summer, and there's no place to go fishing or anything," Heidi said. "I'm not sure I'm gonna like it here. What am . . ."

The squeal of bicycle brakes interrupted her thought. A biker stopped in front of the school alongside Heidi. The rider took off her helmet and shook out a lion-like head of red hair. A slim yet strong-looking woman smiled at Heidi. Her face was lightly freckled, and she had hazel eyes that Heidi found inviting.

"Are you going to be a student here next term?" the woman asked.

"Yes, ma'am. I guess."

"You don't seem too sure," the woman chuckled.

"We moved here from Cumberland, Maine, and, well . . . I don't know anybody or what kids do around here."

"I see," the woman said. "Well, I'm a teacher here at Samuel Tucker. What grade will you be in when September rolls around?"

"The third grade, ma'am. I'll be eight soon."

"That's the grade I teach. But our school has more than one of every grade. Who knows? Perhaps we'll be learning together next term."

"That would be nice," Heidi said.

"By the way, my name is Nancy. Ms. Pelligree. But you can call me Nancy. What's yours?"

"Heidi. Heidi Morgan."

"Well, pleased to meet you, Heidi Morgan."

Heidi stood still, arms to her sides, not sure what to make of this seemingly kind person. Head tilted ever so slightly to the right, she wondered if all the teachers were so friendly.

"Now, back to your problem," Nancy said, furrowing her brow. "What are we going to do about you?"

"Do about me? I don't understand."

"Well, we can't have you moping around all summer. Do you own a bicycle?"

"Yeah, sure."

"Well, would you like to take a ride with me to the animal shelter?"

"Sure! But I'll have to ask my mom first."

"Of course. So, what are we waiting for?"

Before allowing Heidi to go off with a stranger, Helen took the precaution of checking Nancy's credentials and calling the animal shelter. "You can't be too careful," she said to Nancy, who agreed that caution was best. Their short conversation ended with a handshake and friendly smiles.

The ride to the shelter took them eastward through streets lined with townhouses. A quick right followed by two left turns put them on Deer Run Court. Heidi and Nancy rode it all the way to the baseball diamond. Then they took a path circling around to a wooden bridge that crossed the Holmes Run River, followed by a ride down Holmes Run Trail to their destination, the Animal Welfare League of Alexandria.

"C'mon in," Nancy said. "I volunteer here, so I have the run of the place. At least most of it."

Heidi stepped inside and spun around slowly, taking everything in. "Where do they keep the dogs for adoption?"

"C'mon, I'll show you."

They passed through well-worn double doors. Heidi could hear dogs barking, and the smell of dog permeated the hallway. She didn't mind a bit. They walked down a long corridor with cages on both sides. Heidi saw dogs of all shapes and sizes. Some were alert and others, it seemed, had given up hope.

The excitement of being there mixed with a dull ache as the reality these dogs faced, if not adopted, became obvious. It sent a chill through Heidi. Three cages down, on the left, spaced away from the other dogs, a little black puppy was coughing. His cage had fresh vomit in it, and he barely looked up when Heidi and Nancy came closer.

"What's wrong with him?" Heidi asked. "Why does he look so terrible?"

One of the attendants heard Heidi and walked toward her shaking her head. "Yes, regrettably, we may have to put this little guy down."

"No, give him a chance," Heidi pleaded.

"There's not much we can do. He might have distemper."

"You said 'might.' You don't know for sure?"

"No, but . . ."

"Wait. Let me take him home and take care of him, at least until he's better. Maybe it's not distemper. Maybe I can nurse him back to health."

"You mean foster him?" Nancy asked.

"Yeah, foster him."

"You'll need your parents' permission, and fast," the attendant said. "He's scheduled for the vet tomorrow afternoon."

"Okay, I'll come back in the morning." Heidi looked up at the attendant. "Would it be okay if I stay with him for a little while?"

"Yes, of course. Would you be willing to clean out his cage and put down fresh paper?"

"Sure," Heidi said. "Tell me where everything is, and I'll get right to it. My dad says people who get right to it are the people who make a difference."

"You have a wise father," Nancy said. "I look forward to meeting him one day."

Chapter 3: Native American for Bear

That night, after dinner, Heidi helped clean up. She could tell her mom sensed something was afoot, but she had said nothing. When they were alone, Heidi blurted out her burning question. "Mom, may I foster a little sick puppy? It's just until he gets better or we know for sure he can't be saved."

"Hmm . . . Did you ask your father?"

"No. I thought I'd ask you first."

"Figured as much," Helen chuckled, then called out, "Greg, can you come in here for a minute? Heidi has something to ask us."

"Oh, Mom," Heidi said.

Greg strolled into the kitchen. "What is it?" He sat down at the kitchen table and stared at Heidi. "I hope you haven't gotten into trouble already. Let me go check to see if there are police cars outside."

"*Daaaaad*, this is serious."

"Okay, what's up?"

"I was visiting the animal shelter today with a teacher I met from my new school. Well, there's this little puppy who needs someone to take care of him or . . . or . . . they're going to . . ." Heidi started to cry. She ran to her dad, burying her head in his lap. ". . . they'll kill him, and he's such a cute puppy."

"All right, calm down, we're not going to let a little puppy die unnecessarily."

"If you and Mom write me a note saying I can foster him, they'll let me take him home."

Her parents gave each other a gaze. "Helen," Greg said, "do you know where we . . . or *if* we . . . unpacked the stationary?"

Heidi jumped up and down. "Thanks, Daddy! Thanks, Mom! I can't wait to go get him." She laughed and cried happy tears, then hugged them both and skipped through the house.

The next morning, bright and early, with a signed letter in hand, Heidi and her mom walked through the front door of the animal shelter. Her mom waited while Heidi ran to see her puppy. But when she got to his cage, he was gone. His empty cage drained all her excitement. Heidi fell to her knees, tears streaming down both cheeks.

"What is it, sweetie?" an attendant asked.

"The puppy . . . he's gone. They killed him."

"No! He's here. He's being checked over by the vet before we let you take him home."

Heidi sprang to her feet and wiped her eyes. "Where is he? Can I see him?"

"Yes, of course. Come with me." The attendant held out her hand, and Heidi took hold, skipping down the hall.

After the vet checked the puppy out, he clipped a leash to his collar and said, "Well, here you go. He'll need plenty of care."

"Don't worry, he'll get lots of love," Heidi said.

"Oh, of that I'm sure. But in addition to love, you'll need to give him this medication with his food. Let us know how he's doing and call if you have questions. Remember he might not get better so be prepared for that."

"I know, but maybe if a take real good care of him..." Heidi didn't finish her thought not wanting to jinx it.

Once home and under Heidi's care, the puppy became stronger with each day that passed. The little black dog had a few things wrong, but he did not have distemper. It wasn't long before Heidi was plumping him up; he had been all skin and bones when she first brought him home. Now he played and romped around endlessly.

She named him Mato, the word for "bear" in a Native American language she'd read about, because he looked like a bear cub. One of Mato's favorite foods was peanut butter. When the jar was almost empty, Heidi let him stick his nose in it and lick out all the remains.

One evening, a week or so later, Heidi's dad turned to her mom and, with a twinkle in his eye, said, "You know, I think instead of giving Mato back, we should adopt him and make this his forever home. What do you think?"

"Yes," Helen said, "I've become very fond of him. What do you say, Heidi? Should we keep him?"

"Oh. *Oh!* For real? You mean it? Forever? Oh, you guys are the best!"

Tears streaming down her face, Heidi ran to Mato and hugged him so tightly that Helen said, "Careful. His stuffing will come out."

Once again, Heidi laughed and laughed, and

cried happy tears, then laughed and cried some more.

"Of course, you'll have to keep taking care of him," her dad said.

"I will," Heidi said. "You know I will. C'mon, Mato, let's celebrate."

Heidi gave Mato his favorite chew bone. Then they practiced all the things she had taught him.

Chapter 4: The Open House

Although it was a short bike ride to the animal shelter, Heidi's mom did not let her ride there alone. "It's too dangerous, my sweet girl," she told her. "We're not in Cumberland anymore. You have to be more careful here. C'mon, I'll drive you over."

"Can we take my bike so I can ride home with Ms. Pelligree if she says it's okay?" Heidi asked.

"All right, as long as you ride with an adult."

From that day on, Heidi went to the shelter every chance she got. Some days, she brought Mato with her.

One day, Linda, a lady who worked at the shelter said, "I've been meaning to ask. How did you come up with the name Mato?"

While Heidi and Linda talked, they walked down a row of cages that needed cleaning. "Well," Heidi said, "when he was much smaller, and even now sometimes, he looks like a bear cub."

Linda stared at Mato. "Yeah, I can see that."

"I looked up the word some Native American people use for bear, and Mato was it."

"Hmm, how interesting. By the way, are you coming to the open house on Sunday?" Linda asked.

"Yes, I'm planning to. Do you know if Nancy will be there?"

"Yes, I'm sure of it. She teaches at the school you go to, right?" Heidi nodded, and Linda added, "From what I hear, she's a terrific teacher. Will you be in her class this September?"

"I don't know for sure," Heidi said, "but she does teach third grade, so maybe."

"Well, listen, we're about finished here. Why don't you call your mom and have her pick you guys up? You can leave your bike so you and Nancy can ride home together on Sunday," Linda suggested.

"Oh, that's a wonderful idea, thanks," Heidi said. "Okay, if you're sure you don't need my help, I'll see you Sunday."

"I'm sure. See you Sunday." Linda said. "And remember we're having pizza delivered so come hungry."

"Will do. Bye"

On the night of the open house, Heidi patted Mato on the head before she left. "You stay home and behave," she told him. "This party is to help find forever homes for other dogs. You already have your forever home. Do you understand?"

Mato tilted his head and lay down, then rolled over, asking for a chest and tummy rub, which Heidi granted.

"All right, boy, gotta go," Heidi said. "I won't be too long."

The shelter had put out word they were having an open house. People from all around the area came. A small crowd started to fill the yard. Workers already had tables set up with brochures and stood ready to answer questions, smiles on their faces. They gave folks tours and, of course, hoped for adoptions, with papers at the ready.

Along with the brochures tables, shelter staff put out a table with an assortment of drinks and another with boxes of everybody's favorite food: pizza. The pies, stacked in three piles, included plain, mushroom, and pepperoni. Aromas from the freshly delivered pizza filled the shelter's outdoor event space. But the smell of fresh baked pizza did not stop there. It flowed through the neighborhood and out over a sizable perimeter, mostly to the north.

Temptation from the pie's flavorful smell would be hard to resist for any dog, even during the best of times. This was not the best of times for a dog without a home. Pizza was a temptation a stray, hungry, young, and growing American Bulldog could not resist. With abandonment, a white, short-haired muscular body bounded into the yard. The group of visitors lining up for pizza jumped back, startled, and amazed.

A box of pepperoni pizza was open, and the Bulldog ran toward it, ignoring all the people and animals. He had only one objective: to get that pizza! All the visitors could see was a white blur as the dog made a beeline for the pizza. Simultaneously, the guests made a beeline for the parking lot but were quickly called back. Meanwhile, the Bulldog chomped on slices of pizza, chewing up the pepperoni as fast as he could. It must have tasted *soooo* good.

When Heidi saw what was going on, she realized that the big old dog wasn't being aggressive or threatening—he was just starved. The smell of pizza had called to him.

Turning back, Heidi slowly approached the Bulldog. Pizza hung out of his mouth, and red sauce dotted his nose, which made him seem a little clownlike.

Heidi laughed, "Hey, boy, you were just hungry, weren't you?" She reached out to him gently. "I understand, boy. You were so hungry you simply could not resist the temptation. Am I right?"

The Bulldog greeted Heidi not with growls but with a lick on the hand, along with a tongue-smiling face and a wagging tail. He seemed to be saying, "Hi, and thanks for the pizza!"

The Bulldog's ingratiating gaze was enough for Heidi. She suspected they would fast become friends while he waited for a family to adopt him.

By this time, workers from the shelter had come to examine the dog and snap a leash on his collar. Heidi noticed a tag attached poorly, almost falling off. "Maybe this will tell us who owns him."

Linda came over and gave the tag a closer look. "Hmm, all it says is Franklin. Must be his name."

After taking three or four steps backward, Heidi stared at the dog and in a clear, strong voice, called to him. "Franklin. Come."

The powerful yet playful beast yanked on the leash, and he and Linda lurched forward at full speed before making an abrupt stop at Heidi's feet. "Yup, that's his name, all right," Heidi chuckled.

Linda was not amused. "Okay, enough excitement for one day. I'll get this rascal inside, and we can all get back to our event."

Heidi started to follow, but Linda waved her off. "Heidi, please stay out here and help with the visitors. You have such a good way with folks."

The double message confused her: Stay away, and you're a great help? "Can both coexist? I guess," Heidi whispered to herself.

Chapter 5: Finding Franklin's Owner

A week passed, then two. The shelter tried hard to find Franklin's owner. They posted signs with his photo, asked around the neighborhood, and put ads in the local newspaper, but nothing worked. When Heidi took him on walks, she went in several directions from the shelter and probably covered miles, but no luck.

The shelter's veterinarian, along with Heidi and a few of the various workers and volunteers, tried to determine what kind of dog Franklin was. He was certainly a mix, but no one could be sure of what breeds. They all agreed he was part American Bulldog. But what else? Doggo, perhaps? Pit Bull? Some mix of Bulldog and Labrador? Although they were curious, it was not as important to them as finding him a good home.

One Friday evening, weeks after the open house, Heidi walked through the kennel, Mato heeling at her side. Linda was cleaning the cage opposite Franklin's. When Heidi reached Franklin, she stopped. She noticed that he had light brown spots, which she had somehow missed before. His short white hair, enormous head, and Bulldog stance gave him an impressive appearance. A deep chest and one extra cute brown spot around his nose added to his charm. He gave off a hearty double bark, then sat at attention and panted while Heidi stood smiling at him.

"Holy cow, I never saw him react to anybody like that," Linda said.

Heidi stared into Franklin's eyes. With a slight whimper, he lay down, but remained in an alert stance, his front and back legs ready to advance if asked.

"Why is he still here?" Heidi asked. "Who wouldn't want to keep this guy?"

"No one told you?"

Heidi whirled around to face Linda, who was cleaning one of the dog cages. "Told me what?"

"Apparently he was rescued, sort of, by three college girls who found him in a gas station in Texas. The owner was giving a litter of pups away, and they took this guy home. But a few months later, the little puppy became a full-sized dog and was getting bigger every week. Not too long after that, they admitted they couldn't take care of what had become a huge dog. They released him and went home for the summer. A woman who lived near the girls called us when she saw one of our posters hanging in a coffee shop. To make a long story short, Franklin ended up here."

"Idiots!" Heidi snapped. "Oh, sorry . . . but I mean . . . to just release him? How cruel. I think he's cute. I mean in a manly way. He has class. Don'tcha think?"

"Yes, but he also has a problem." Linda shook her head. "He is part Bulldog and maybe Pit Bull, too. Folks are wary of those breeds. It's a long shot he'll be adopted before his time runs out."

"Well, how long is that?" Heidi cringed, waiting for the answer.

"Unfortunately, not long. Two weeks at best."

"Well, that's not fair. He's a terrific dog, just look at him. Anybody can tell he'd be a wonderful dog to have."

Linda stepped into the walkway between the rows of cages. She assumed Heidi would follow her down to the next cage, but Heidi didn't move. Linda gazed back at her. "Are you thinking what I think you're thinking?"

"Well, if nobody adopts him, I could foster him until we can find him a forever home?"

"A-ha, that's the story you're going with?" Linda asked.

An impish grin curled the corners of Heidi's mouth. "Well, for now, anyway."

Chapter 6: Room for One More

That night, Heidi tried to convince her parents that Mato needed a friend to play with. "He'll be lonely once I go back to school. I promise to spend the rest of the summer training them both. Whaddaya say, Mom? Dad?"

"Let her have him, Greg," her mom said. "She had to leave all her friends, and the dogs are helping her with the transition. Frankly, they'll help me, too. I'll feel safer with the dogs in the house."

"Well, then," Greg said, "I guess we're gonna be a two-dog family."

Heidi hugged her dad, then her mom, and skipped to the back door.

That was easier than I thought it would be.

She immediately put a leash on Franklin before bringing him in to meet Mato. She had brought Franklin home with her and hidden him out back, hoping her dad would give the okay for him to stay.

She already knew her mom was okay with the idea.

After a little getting-to-know-you time, Mato and Franklin settled into a rhythm. To train both dogs would be a challenge, but Mato knew most of the basic commands and would be a huge help. Besides, Franklin already sat and gave his paw. The "come" command would be more difficult, but the dogs were smart and enjoyed working, especially for treats. Heidi was confident she could do it.

Within the span of three weeks, Heidi made unmistakable progress training the two dogs. And it wasn't long before she had another surprise to spring on her parents. Once again, her dad came home from work tired but cheerful—that is, until he was ambushed in his own home. *Three* dogs romped and played while Heidi laughed as she made each dog give her a high-five; they filled the living room with joy.

When Greg saw the four of them playing, he put his hand on his forehead and said, "Oh, no, Heidi. Not three!"

"He's a great dog, Daddy, and he won't be a bit

of trouble, you'll see." Heidi pleaded, hoping against all odds her dad would say yes to Bruce Wayne living with them.

Greg stared at his wife with question marks in his eyes. "What was I to do?" Helen shrugged. "When I pulled up in front of the shelter, Heidi was waiting with this large black-and-brown dog sitting next to her." Helen looked down at Heidi lovingly. "She was so happy. Right away, she told me how she wanted to foster him so they wouldn't euthanize the poor guy. Apparently, someone badly neglected him. He was all scrawny when the rescuers found him, but he's fine now. I think he'll be a faithful dog."

Greg sighed and shook his head. "But three, sweetie, really?"

"I promise I'll never ask for anything ever again," Heidi said, patting Bruce on the head. "He's such a good boy, and they . . . well, you know, his time was up, and nobody adopted him. I . . . I mean *we* would be saving his life. And I'll take care of him just like I have the other dogs, I promise."

"She has been very responsible taking care of Mato and Franklin," Helen said. "I think having these dogs taught her a lot about responsibility and caring for others, too." Leaning over, she whispered in Greg's ear, "Both are important lessons."

"Oh, if you two don't beat all. Where did this diggity-dog get the name Bruce Wayne?"

"The people at the shelter didn't know his name," Heidi said, "but somebody said he looked like a cave dog and, well . . ."

"Well, I never could say no to my special girls," Greg said. "All right, but no more dogs! And you promise to take care of him and keep him only until someone adopts him, right?" Greg knew full well the odds were they would be a three-dog family forever.

"Woohoo. Oh, thank you, Daddy. You won't be sorry. I promise."

Upon hearing Greg give the okay, Bruce Wayne, a Rottweiler mix breed, gave him a dog kiss on the ear and leaned against Greg to let him know he trusted him. Heidi watched as her dad put his hand on the dog's head. "You're a handsome guy. I guess you deserve a break, aye fella."

Pleased and relieved, Heidi ran to her dad and threw her arms around his neck. She giggled happily as a tear meandered down the side of her face.

"My daughter the dog whisper," he said laughing. His comment earned him another big hug and a twinkle in Heidi's eye.

In the days and weeks that followed, Heidi was good to her word. She took care of all three dogs. She trained them, fed them, walked them, cleaned up after them, and most importantly, she loved them.

And they loved her back.

Book 2 (excerpt): *Heidi and the Three Bullies*

One weekend in September, Heidi and the hounds were out walking. Franklin had just lifted a leg to relieve himself when Heidi spied what appeared to be kids arguing. When Franklin was done, she continued walking and watching the five kids with interest. The dogs' ears perked up too.

"C'mon, boys, let's find out what's going on," Heidi said, and a faster pace ensued.

The closer Heidi and the dogs came, the more she could hear, and she didn't like what she heard. A big-bellied boy and his two friends were mocking two girls about Heidi's age. The mocking seemed cruel. Heidi didn't know what she could do, but she kept walking and listening, the dogs heeling alongside her.

One of the boys, the big-bellied one, said, "Hey, you're skinnier than a toothpick. Don't your mama never feed you nothin'?"

A taller boy said, "And look at this one," pointing to the other girl. "You look like ya neva stop eatin'."

They all laughed. The heavier of the two girls tried hard to hold back tears. The boys' laughter was hurtful.

"Come over here, let me see what's in your bag," said the big-bellied kid, holding out his hand, ready to grab the other girl's belongings.

"No, these are my things." the thinner of the two girls said.

"Correction, they *were* your things. Now they're mine."

The girl pulled her bag back, but the boy laughed. "Hand it over, or we'll take it. Trust me, you won't like how." He made a fist and shook it in her face, his eyes and mouth contorted into an angry, pugnacious mask.

The taller boy echoed his friend's threat, flashing a nasty grin and high-fiving the third boy. "Take it. What she gonna do?"

About the Author

Carey V. Azzara is no stranger to twists and turns, overcoming life challenges on route to obtaining two graduate degrees and establishing a successful career spanning public health and market research—all while raising a family and rescuing a few dogs. He has published articles, reports, and books, writing for the joy of sharing his ideas and stories with his readers.

Azzara authored *Halley's Gift and Eight Other Extraordinary Tales*, *Uncommon Heroes & Cars*, *The Lottery Curse*, and *Kaitlin's Mooring*. He also wrote the children's book *Ready or Not, Here We Come!* and several short stories published in Storyacious and the anthology *Swallowed by the Beast*.

Forthcoming works include *Forever Damaged*, *Clydesdales on Cobblestones*, and *Halley's Gift: The Adventure Begins*.

About the Publisher

Glass Spider Publishing is an independent publisher located in Ogden, Utah. The company was founded by writer Vince Font to help underrepresented authors gain visibility. Visit www.glassspiderpublishing.com to learn more.

Made in the
USA
Middletown, DE